SCHOLASTIC INC.
New York Toronto London Auckland
Sydney Mexico City New Delhi Hong Kong

Duck! Rabbit!

AMY KROUSE ROSENTHAL & TOM LICHTENHELD

Hey, look! A duck!

Are you kidding me?
It's totally a duck.

It's for sure a rabbit.

See, there's his bill.

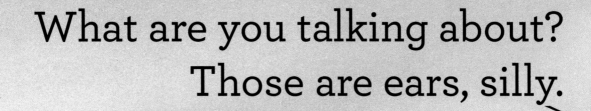

What are you talking about?
Those are ears, silly.

It's a duck. And he's about to eat a piece of bread.

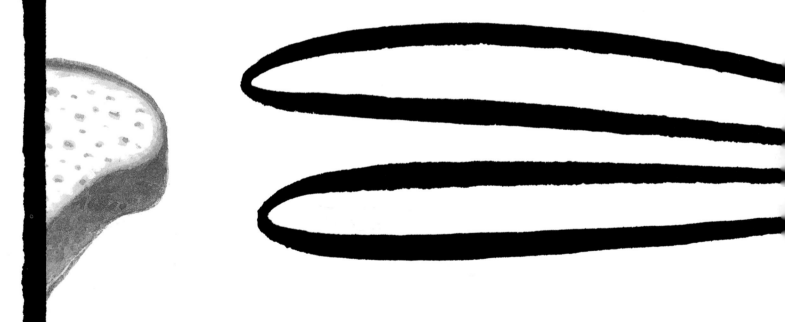

It's a rabbit. And he's about to eat a carrot.

Wait. Listen. Did you hear that?
I heard duck sounds.

Now the duck is wading through the swamp.

Here,
look at
the duck
through my
binoculars.

Sorry,
still a
rabbit.

Here, ducky ducky!

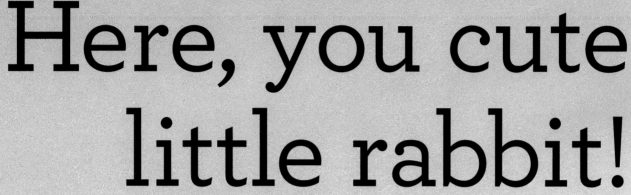

Oh great, you scared him away.

I didn't scare him away.
You scared him away.

You know, maybe you were right. Maybe it *was* a rabbit.

Thing is, now I'm actually thinking it was a duck.

Well, anyway...now what
do you want to do?

I don't know. What do *you* want to do?

The End.